A *Gift*
FOR THE
Christmas
DRAGON

A *Gift* FOR THE *Christmas* DRAGON

MARIE CARDNO
WRITING AS
ZOE CHANT

1

ABIGAIL

It was a month before Christmas, and if something did not change soon, Abigail Heartwell was going to lose her goddamn mind.

Luckily, it was book club night.

She slammed her hands on the table. "I have a problem."

The other members of the book club stared at her. Her stomach flip-flopped from nerves—but she couldn't stay quiet about this any longer.

Anyway, these were all the closest friends she'd made since that wonderful Christmas six years ago when she had found her soulmate and her own happiness after a lifetime of loneliness.

There was Meaghan, the human alpha of the local hellhound pack. Her twins weren't even two yet, and she still looked fresher than Abigail felt with only one kid, probably because Meaghan's little ones had a pack of big fiery dogs to take them on adventures and get them out of their mom's hair when she needed a break.

Sheena, a former sheep shifter from New Zealand who through a series of way too exciting events had become a hellsheep shifter, had been quieter than normal all evening, and was sticking to non-alcoholic drinks in a way that everyone else was being careful not to comment on. She jumped when Abigail hit the table and pretended she hadn't been dozing off.

Olly, who was hosting tonight's meeting, was in the kitchen getting treats out of the oven, but Abigail didn't fool herself that meant she would miss what she said next. Olly's inner owl heard *everything*.

If they couldn't help her…

She gritted her teeth. "And I need your help."

Delphine, the newest member of their book club, blinked. "With the book?"

Delphine was probably the only one of them who'd actually *read* the book.

"Not with the book," Abigail admitted.

"Uh-oh." Meaghan leaned forward. "How can we—"

"No time to beat around the bush. I have to tell you now, before Opal gets here." Opal was the final member of their book club.

And Abigail's sister-in-law.

She drew a deep breath. It still felt unnatural to ask anyone for help—but these were her friends. They'd been there with her through every new, wonderful turn her life had taken.

Also, she was desperate.

She closed her eyes briefly, focusing on the golden bond of light that connected her to her husband. Jasper was her fated mate—something she hadn't even known existed until she met him and he turned into a dragon right in front of her. The mate bond was invisible to the eye but clear to the heart. It shone with all the love they had for one another. If she concentrated, she could sense her mate's emotions through it.

She concentrated now, just to be extra sure.

And there it was. Beneath the warm, slightly tinsel-y glow was a twitch of something that made her own heart tighten. Stress, anxiety, worry—she couldn't put a name to it, but it was *there.*

Something was worrying Jasper, *her* Jasper, and he wasn't talking to her about it.

There could be only one reason for that.

She braced herself. "You all know that Christmas is *extremely* important to Jasper."

Everyone nodded. Meaghan, who'd known her and Jasper the longest, started to look concerned.

"It's important to me as well! You know, I don't hate it anymore. But—" She hesitated, fretting her fingers together.

"What did you say about no time for beating around the bush?" Meaghan asked teasingly.

Abigail opened her mouth and found herself avoiding the point again. "You all know what he's like. He spends every holiday season like he's trying to put Santa Claus out of a job. He works so hard to make the holidays magical for everyone. He'll be up all night, making sure everything's *perfect*. And it is! Christmas in Pine Valley is incredible, and it's because he puts so much work into making that happen."

She paused again.

"But…?" Meaghan prompted her.

"But—" She broke off.

The other women exchanged a glance.

"It's his birthday too, isn't it?" Sheena said. "I remember Fleance saying. Jasper Heartwell, the Christmas dragon."

Delphine put her chin on her hands and narrowed her eyes. "And you two got together at Christmas, so that makes it your anniversary."

"Ah-ha! And you want to keep him up all night, every night, busy with something else?" Sheena suggested with a grin.

"What?!" Abigail squeaked. "No, I—"

"You want us to help you get some!" Olly exclaimed with delight from behind her.

Abigail jumped in her seat. "Eek!"

"Eek and yes?" Olly asked placidly. "Cookie?"

Abigail took one of the still-warm cinnamon cookies from the plate Olly offered her, feeling tongue-tied. "Eek and, well…"

"Why didn't you say something earlier?" Meaghan asked.

"I can guess. Because Christmas is Jasper's *thing*, and she doesn't want to ruin it for him," Delphine suggested.

"And you thought you could white-knuckle your way through the next month unsatisfied and unfulfilled?" Sheena added before Abigail could answer.

"Hey! I am *satisfied.* And—stop laughing! That's not it, but thanks for proving that everyone's going to *think* it is, and—we have to come up with a plan before Opal gets here!"

"You have to do what before I get here?"

Abigail's heart fell into her stomach. She didn't want to talk to Opal about it, because Opal had already spent too much of her life worried about Jasper and the family curse that had come so close to claiming him.

She made a quick *shush* gesture to the rest of the table, and every single one of her so-called friends grinned evilly.

She covered her face as Opal sat down next to her and the others caught her up.

"Embarrassed?" Opal asked, leaning in for a hug. "Because you're in love with my dumbass kid brother and want to make sure he knows it?"

I mean, also that. Not a day goes by that I don't want to pin him to the bed for at least half the day—not that we've been able to do that in a few years. She gnawed on her lower lip.

Maybe it was better if Opal thought her issue was Jasper being too busy with Christmas to pin her to her bed as much as she wanted, rather than that he was hiding some deep, dark secret.

And… maybe that *was* part of the problem, anyway? For real?

She and Jasper had a dream life. A beautiful home, amazing friends and family, and a daughter who brought joy and chaos into every room she set foot in. Jasper wasn't only the love of her life, he was her fated mate. Her soulmate. It was a magical connection that even as a non-magical human she could feel, a bond of extraordinary power and love.

Which was a long-winded way of saying that six years into their relationship, she *still* wanted to get down every chance they got, and chances were thin on the ground this time of year with how busy they both were.

"Um," she said out loud. "Yes. Kind of. That's some of it! But also—you know how he gets around Christmas, and this year it's like…"

"Like you barely get to see him at all?" Opal gave her a sympathetic smirk. "All right. Forget this week's book. Project Abigail Gets the Anniversary She Deserves is all go."

Everyone raised their mugs in a toast. Abigail joined them, ducking her head with a grimace of embarrassment and a flicker of guilt.

Because as much as she wanted some alone time with her husband, that wasn't the only reason she wanted her friends to conspire to take a load off Jasper's shoulders.

She was worried about him.

2

JASPER

"I need your help," Jasper said to his friends, "to make this Christmas the best Christmas ever."

They were all hanging out in hellhound shifter Caine's front room, with a fire blazing in the fireplace and the credits for a kids' cartoon playing on the TV.

The kids themselves were scattered around the furniture: Jasper's daughter Ruby was playing under the table, determined to stay awake as long as the grown-ups, while Caine's twins Lola and Hamish were fast asleep sprawled over him, pinning him to the sofa.

Every month when their mates had their book club, the guys got together for a pizza and movie night with the kids and, after the kids were asleep, a poker night for them. And tonight, same as every month, nobody was even sure where the poker stuff was, and they'd all been more invested in watching the cartoon than they would like to admit.

Jasper's nephew Cole would normally be home with his dad while mom Opal was at book club, but Hank was out of town. Unimpressed by the cartoon on offer, he had disappeared in a pre-teen huff to do important pre-teen stuff in the kitchen… which probably meant Caine would be due an emergency grocery trip in the morning.

And Christmas was only a month away.

The knowledge itched under his skin. He wanted to fly home and dive into the plans he'd been making for this year—but it wasn't that simple.

"Uh-huh." Griffin shifter Hardwick was the grumpy, silent type, and his expression spoke far more eloquently than his grumbling. "That right?"

Griffin shifter. Jasper's inner dragon shifted its wings uncomfortably, but Jasper didn't need the warning. Griffins could tell when people were lying, but he wasn't lying. "I want this year to be the best Christmas ever," he repeated.

Hardwick's eyes narrowed, but he didn't say anything.

Because Jasper was telling the truth.

Wasn't he?

"Don't you want *every* year to be the best Christmas ever?" Caine asked from somewhere beneath the two toddlers using him as a mattress.

"Of course. But this year is—" Jasper hesitated.

"Your, what, six-year anniversary?" Caine suggested. He counted under his breath. "You two got together the year before Meaghan and I met, right?"

On the other couch, pegasus shifter Jackson snapped his fingers. "And it's your birthday! Dude, you're sneakier than Olly. Forget Christmas—"

"That's not what's important!"

The others stared. One of the twins snuffled and wiggled in their sleep, and Caine's stare snapped into a warning glare.

Jasper raised his hands. "Sorry. But forget my birthday. That's not what's important."

Jasper looked around the group of friends. He'd spent most of his teenaged and adult life away from Pine Valley, traveling the world searching for his fated mate—and failing to find her until he gave up and returned home.

He'd always been outgoing—you had to be, when you were in a new town every couple of weeks—but now, for the first time in his life, he had more actual friends than he knew what to do with.

Caine and Fleance, the hellhound shifters who'd had to come to terms with their own curses, the same way he'd almost given up ever breaking his. Jackson, who'd only discovered later in life that he was a shifter—and whose life had turned upside down because of it. And Hardwick, whose ability to sense lies was so… fine, absolutely fine, because who was lying? Not him.

He spread his arms. "It's Christmas, and… look, we all know how I get around Christmas, right? I'm the Christmas dragon! It's the most magical time of the year. And this year I want to make sure it's the most magical time of *any* year."

Fleance rubbed his chin and frowned. "How much more magical can it get? There's already the Christmas tree village with Santa in the town square, the combination sleigh-ride-and-Santa-letters thing, the best dressed house competition, the Christmas Eve choir… Do you need our help doing more, or less?"

Not less. Jasper's chest tightened. He couldn't do *less Christmas.*

"I can handle those," Jasper said off-handedly, and Fleance's eyebrows got lost somewhere in his long hair. "I was thinking we could add something to them, though. What if—"

He rattled off a few ideas.

The others stared at him.

"He's lost it," Hardwick deadpanned. "Honestly. You can't think of anything else you'd rather be doing?"

Jasper's mind went straight to his soulmate. His gorgeous, perfect Abigail, still sometimes as prickly as the day he'd met her and all the sweeter for it. All her life, Christmas had been a source of tension and unhappiness, not a time for celebration.

And his little girl. Ruby was old enough now to look forward to Christmas from the minute Halloween was over. And she didn't have the same bittersweet relationship to it as he used to. She was a summer baby, and one of the best things in his life. Sharing the magic of the holidays with her made them more magical every year.

Which was why this had to be the best year ever. For them.

"Nope," he said in confident response to Hardwick's question. "Nothing. And stop squinting at me like that. We've got work to do."

Jackson folded his arms. "We haven't said yes, yet."

Jasper waited. And just as he'd hoped, his friends stepped in.

"All right, Christmas dragon. You spend half your year making sure Christmas is incredible for everyone else in this town, we ought to step in and help out. What do you need?"

3

ABIGAIL

Pine Valley at Christmas used to be everything Abigail hated. Christmas *anywhere* used to be anything she hated. But somehow it was this cute little town that threw itself heart and soul into the holiday season that changed her own heart.

Or rather, one Christmas-obsessed dragon shifter who lived there.

These days, she loved it. The decorations. The market in the town square. The smell of cinnamon and pine. The carols.

Yes, even the carols. Now that she wasn't trapped behind a cash register with the same crackly off-brand recordings playing all day long, she could appreciate even them.

And so many other people loved it too. Thanks to all the hard work Jasper put into the public celebrations.

Was she really going to put all that at risk?

Don't be ridiculous, she told herself as she packed a bag for the evening. *I'm not going to ruin Christmas! I just…am going to steal it… a little…*

She bit back a sigh, remembering a fleeting look of tension in Jasper's eyes that morning as he stared at their Christmas tree. It was the biggest one they'd ever had in all the Christmases they'd spent together, and she'd joked that if they were going to top it next year, they'd need to add another floor to their house.

He'd grinned like it was a challenge, but the golden bond in her heart had *pinched.*

The problem was obvious. He was overworking himself. Even if he wouldn't admit it. She wasn't going to ruin Christmas. She was going to help her husband, her *fated mate,* relax and enjoy himself.

And get some.

Oh, lord, was she going to get some.

Heat flared with unexpected speed across her skin, and she squeezed her legs together. It wasn't that they *never* had any time together. It was just that somehow, she was… extra horny?

She blamed Sheena for putting the idea in her head.

"Everyone ready to go?" she hollered as she headed for the front door, and Jasper bounded down the stairs. He and Ruby were in matching Christmas elf outfits. The same as she was, because she was a part of this crazy Christmas-loving family, after all.

Even if she was going to ruin Christmas.

I'm not going to ruin anything! She snapped at herself and jingled the keys. "Race you to the car!"

The town square could have been designed to hold the Christmas market. For all Abigail knew, it really had been.

Every shop front was ablaze with lights and festive decorations. Christmas trees in wine-barrel planters had been rolled into the plaza, creating a mock forest through which tinsel-y paths wove in and out between food trucks and picnic areas. There was a big open space with a stage, where the local choir would be singing, and it smelled like a festive feast in an enchanted, snowy grove.

The Christmas market opened each year with a small ceremony, early enough in the evening for kids to enjoy. Jasper kissed Abigail and Ruby and bounded up on stage to begin the official festivities. There were speeches by Jasper and local business owners, spot-prizes for best dressed and best Christmas-themed heckling, and finally Jasper relinquished the stage to the local choir, to sing in the holiday season.

He picked up Ruby and swung her onto his shoulders. Dwarfed by them both, Abigail leaned against him and let out a happy sigh. "This is so lovely. Just like last year," she said happily.

"Just like?" Jasper echoed.

Was she imagining things, or did he sound almost disappointed?

"Can we get donut sticks again like last year?" Ruby asked, wide-eyed.

"You betcha," Abigail told her. "You remember them?"

"You said that this year I can have five, because I'm five!"

"First of all, you're four and a half. Second, I definitely did not… but I'm willing to negotiate." She cracked her knuckles with a grin. "We can start there first, and then check out the—Jasper?"

He offered her a winning smile that made her heart drop.

"I… may have to sneak away for a bit," he admitted.

"What are you planning?" she asked, and didn't like the tone of warning that snuck into her voice.

"Only wonderful things," he promised her. "Look, there's Caine and Meaghan!"

"Look, there's Jasper and Abigail," Meaghan retorted, walking up to them with a grin. She leaned in for a hug and Abigail got a bonus, sticky-mittened hug from the toddler strapped to her back. Caine followed a moment later, the other twin slung over one shoulder, cackling wildly. "The Christmas market looks amazing this year! You guys heading over to get some food?"

"And…" Jasper's eyes flicked conspiratorially to Caine.

And Meaghan's eyes snapped to meet Abigail's. She nodded sharply. Neither of them had shifter telepathic abilities, but right now, they didn't need them.

Operation Save-or-Steal-or-*Utterly-Destroy*-Christmas was go.

"And what? What are you two up to?" Meaghan prodded her husband in the chest.

"Well—"

"What's happening?" The rest of the hellhound pack had caught up to them, and Sheena was leading the charge. "Hey, Abigail, Jasper, Ruby, how are you guys going?"

"We're—"

"Ooh, who said something about fireworks?" Sheena exclaimed, and Abigail figured someone had just totally failed at keeping a telepathic whisper quiet enough. Sheena grinned. "What do you need us to do?"

"I was going to—" Jasper began.

"Nuh-uh. Fireworks are hellhound business. And hellsheep business."

"I breathe fire!" He glanced sideways and winced as a few probably-not-shifter festival-goers gave him an odd look. "Ahem. Metaphorically speaking."

Sheena folded her arms. "And we can *stop* them. Which I feel like is more important for last-minute, amateur fireworks displays. *You* enjoy the Christmas village." She gave Abigail a 'subtle' hip-bump shove towards Jasper. "So, what was the plan? We just let them off, or…? Do you need a license for it? Ooh, what if we turned it into a Santa thing? Jackson and Hardwick can fly…"

"We can what?" The rest of their group had arrived: Olly and Jackson, and Delphine and Hardwick. Hardwick's expression darkened as the others caught him up.

Meaghan nudged her. "This is your chance to escape," she murmured. "Want me to take Ruby on the pony rides?"

"Ooh, Jackson can do pony rides, too!"

"I think you'll find I can't," Jackson tried in vain to point out.

Meanwhile, Hardwick was growling, "I may be able to fly, but I also have very strong views on fire safety—"

Abigail looked up at her husband. She took his hand, and he shook himself as though coming out of a dream.

"Donuts?" she suggested.

An expression of something close to regret flickered over his face, and her chest tightened.

"This wasn't what I—" he began, but Ruby interrupted.

"Donuts!" she declared. "I get FIVE."

She clambered down from his shoulders and marched off, leaving them no choice but to hurry after her through the glittering Christmas village.

"Come and find me after you get the donuts!" Meaghan called after them.

"I feel like someone just stole Christmas off me," Jasper complained as they rushed after their determined daughter.

"Maybe they're just excited to help out?" Abigail suggested innocently.

Ruby found the donut truck. And then, with an attention to detail Abigail had never noticed in her before, she found every other food and drink truck in the village. By the time they made it back to the main pavilion, they were laden down with holiday treats and trinkets from the market stalls.

One look at Ruby's shining eyes as she showed her parents all the things she'd bought and listed which of her friends they were for, and Abigail knew there was no chance she was going to take up Meaghan's offer to watch her while she and Jasper snuck off together.

If she could even convince Jasper to sneak off.

Not that that was what this was all about, even if that was what her friends believed.

So, they stayed. They cheered the choir and whooped as fireworks filled the sky. They spent the evening drinking hot chocolate and feasting on food truck treats, and as Abigail watched the reflection of fireworks and fairy lights in her family's eyes, something eased inside her.

Maybe she had been wrong. Jasper wasn't over-working himself over Christmas. She'd got the wrong end of things—probably because of her own lingering Christmas-related issues.

Everything was fine.

4

JASPER

Everything was not fine.

What was all that about last night? he demanded the moment he sensed Caine in telepathic range. He assumed the hellhound was leading one of the dogsled tours around the valley, if he was that close. In human form, of course; they had actual dogs to pull the sleds. Ones that didn't leak sulfur-scented smoke into the air.

What was what about? Caine asked with a psychic laugh.

You jumping in and taking over the fireworks!

Thought you said you wanted help?

I wanted… Jasper groaned. *Yes, help, but…*

He couldn't put it into words. Why couldn't he put it into words? It was obvious. He wanted to make this Christmas the best Christmas ever, to show his mate and his family that—that—

That his mate would never have to make that expression he'd caught in her fleeting glances ever again. The one that she'd worn so often when they first met: small and still and worried. Like she was expecting the world to throw bad things at her.

It had appeared again this Christmas, just as things were starting to ramp up. And when he focused on the shining mate bond that connected his soul to hers, it shivered with unease.

He needed to fix this for her. To give her the perfect holiday season she deserved.

Anyway, Sheena did most of the stealing. You know how her inner hellsheep has more crazy in it than she knows how to deal with. Some controlled explosions were the perfect outlet for all that energy, with Fleance to tease it if it got too distracted. They make a great team.

Caine's telepathic voice was overlaid with a shy sense of pride. Jasper knew he still found it strange, being the alpha of a hellhound pack. But he and Meaghan had taken on their responsibilities with that same sense of pride and determination to do right by the others who were bonded to them by pack status. Even if Fleance and Sheena were on their way to making their own pack.

I guess what I'm saying is, thanks for the opportunity. I owe you one.

Jasper blinked. *You're thanking me?*

Sure. We all had a great time. I think I even saw Hardwick smile. Don't tell him I said so, though.

And you owe me one? Jasper thought fast. *Good, because I have another idea…*

The week raced past. There were the ordinary life things that still had to be done: work, groceries, helping Ruby with her latest madcap schemes, bailing Ruby out of her latest madcap schemes.

Then there were the ordinary Christmas things: helping his friends and family hide their Christmas present shopping from one another through a complicated system of having parcels mailed to each other's houses and picking them up without anyone noticing—always difficult in a small town, more difficult when half the people you knew were psychic and your daughter thought the best part of a surprise was telling everyone about it as soon as possible. Finishing decorating the house, an activity that actually never finished, because every time he stepped out the door, he stepped back inside with a new ornament or idea for a Christmas craft they could make together.

Which was where he'd gotten his latest idea. A way to bring even more Christmas to the *entire* town.

His dragon nosed at him with a huff of sparks. He frowned. Yes, of course, this was a good idea. How could it be a bad one?

"You want to *what*?" Hardwick crossed his arms.

Jasper wasn't even entirely sure why he was having this conversation with Hardwick. "A Christmas tree decorating competition. We've done them before."

"Yes. You've done ones where people send in photos of the trees in their own houses. One year, you did one where people competed in teams to decorate pre-selected trees in the Christmas village."

"This is basically the same as that!"

"Except instead of one tree per team, it's—"

"All the trees in and around town, yes."

Hardwick stared at him. Jasper stared back. Their inner animals stared at each other, too. Admittedly, Jasper's inner dragon had also been slightly hesitant when he first came up with this idea, but the thought of exactly how sparkly and shiny the town would become had won it over.

Hardwick's griffin did not appear to be being won over.

Hardwick dropped his head into his hands, groaning something that sounded like 'health and safety'.

Out loud, he grumbled, "And you want to plan this when, exactly?"

"I've planned it all already—"

"Of course you have." Hardwick raised his head. His eyes narrowed as he cast a strange look at Jasper. "Have you and Abigail actually talked about—"

"Talked about what?" Abigail's cheeks were pink as she came in, and Jasper had a sudden, wonderful memory of the last time he'd made her cheeks go that color. Surely not that long? "Hi, Hardwick!"

"Hi, Abigail. How'd your shopping trip go?"

"In the interests of answering that without lying, I'm going to say it was *almost* all great." Abigail had gone to the next town over—one that was more of a city—to stock up. She flashed Jasper a grin, and he pulled her close for a kiss. "What are you two up to?"

"Planning," Hardwick said flatly.

Abigail stiffened in his arms. "Planning what?"

She sounded as upbeat as before, but Jasper couldn't ignore the way she'd gone tense when Hardwick let the cat out of the bag. Not that he'd let the whole cat out. Barely a whisker.

"Something incredible," he reassured her.

Hardwick made a disbelieving noise.

"Is this what you were up all last night doing?" Abigail asked.

"You caught me."

She sighed and leaned against him. He kept his arms around her, and his dragon imagined wrapping its wings around them both.

"Well, if you didn't sleep all night and you're *still* looking happy about whatever you have planned… it must be a good thing, right?"

There was a hint of uncertainty in her voice. Jasper and his dragon both froze up.

"It's going to be a real party," Hardwick interjected. "Don't worry. We'll make it happen." He checked his watch. "Delphine dropped you off?"

Abigail nodded.

"Then I have just about enough time to grab us dinner and head home while she hides my present." He grinned. "I'll let the others know about the tree decorating plan. Catch you later."

Jasper fought not to let his jaw hang open as Hardwick let himself out. His dragon curled its tail in distress. The Christmas-tree-decorating-town-takeover was *his* idea. If he didn't carry it out, then it wouldn't be *him* making Christmas the best Christmas ever. It wouldn't be…

He swallowed hard, again unable to put into words what was clear in his heart. Abigail looked up at him, a crease between her eyebrows.

"Jasper?"

"My love?"

"I was wondering—" She bit her lip. "Never mind. Tell me about the plan! Or is it a surprise?"

It turned out to be a surprise—for Jasper.

The next morning, they headed out early, but not early enough. By the time they reached the Christmas village in the square, Delphine, Olly, Jackson and Hardwick must have been up for hours.

"Have I got this right?" Abigail murmured to him as Ruby ran ahead to be the first to tackle-hug everyone. "It's a tree decorating competition, but it lasts the whole week, and the challenge is to decorate *literally every pine tree they can reach?*"

"Well, if you say it like that, it sounds unhinged," he joked.

She raised both eyebrows. "Does it?"

"Hardwick thought so." He forced his shoulders not to drop as, inside, his dragon flopped bereft to the ground. "I expect he's managed to turn it into something far more sensible and well-hinged. I'm surprised he took it over, to be honest. I know I asked the guys to help this Christmas—"

"You asked them to help?"

"But—well—there's helping and there's taking over, you know?"

Abigail's mouth moved silently. "Um—maybe I should tell you…"

"There they are!" Meaghan waved them over.

"I'll tell you later," Abigail said quickly, sounding kind of… relieved? "Let's go find out how much they shrunk your original plan." She squeezed his hand, as though she knew he needed comforting about that.

Of course she knew. She was his mate.

"Mommy! Daddy!" Ruby cried out as they got closer. "We're going to decorate EVERY TREE IN THE WHOLE VALLEY!"

Jasper stopped. "Every tree?"

"Every tree!"

Hardwick cleared his throat. "Within a specified perimeter that excludes any area further than twenty feet from an accessible roadway or marked trail," he growled. "Other than that… every tree."

Next to him, Delphine clapped her hands. "And each competing team gets a different theme!"

5

ABIGAIL

By the end of that week, hundreds of locals and visitors had put their artistic talents to the test. Nobody got lost in a snow drift, nobody got injured falling out of a tree, and the town was even more glittering and colorful than it usually was at Christmas.

It was… *really* nice.

And Abigail still hadn't admitted to Jasper that she might be the reason his friends had taken his request to help with Christmas and turned it into taking over Christmas.

Because every time they almost had a moment to themselves, Jasper turned it into a new Christmas plan.

Partway through the tree decorating week, Jasper gathered all their friends together one evening after work and announced a Christmas baking contest.

A *complicated* baking contest.

There were rules. There were sub-rules. There was double-blind taste testing and double-blind judging and double-blind… ingredients?

Abigail held her breath and did some quick mental arithmetic. Looking around the room, it was clear that nobody else was clear on what the rules were, either. Even if Jasper only ran the contest instead of taking part in it as well—and with all the double-blind everything, she got the strong impression that he definitely wanted to compete, as fairly as possible—it would be a huge time investment.

Christmas was a *week* away.

She bit her lip and darted a look at her friends. Meaghan caught her eye and nodded. Operation Help Jasper Take A Break / Help Abigail Get Some was in imminent danger.

Before either of them could say anything, though, Olly interrupted.

"I have a better idea," she said. "*I'll* do all the baking, and *you* all have to eat it and guess what the secret ingredient is."

Abigail was about to object—yes, her friends had offered to help her, but that didn't mean giving up all of their own free time as well—but when she saw how Olly was practically glowing with excitement, she stopped.

Her stomach twisted.

Had she gotten this all wrong?

Her friends were doing more than just help her. They were having fun. They *enjoyed* all the Christmas craziness.

So, what was wrong with her, that she couldn't throw herself into the festivities with them?

She stole a glance at Jasper. He was his usual upbeat self—but there was something distant in his gaze. As though he was already thinking of a replacement for his baking competition idea.

And the bond in her chest pinched unhappily.

As Christmas crept closer, Abigail's worries grew. The scheme wasn't helping. Jasper wasn't relaxing as more things were taken (well, stolen and sneaked) off his plate. Instead, he was finding *more* things to do!

Worst of all, he was his usual cheerful, festive self, bouncing back from every roadblock and avoiding her schemes faster than she could create them—and all the while, the mate bond pinched and ached with a strong sense of *something wrong.*

Only one thing was for sure.

By the time they got to bed each night, they were so Christmassed-out there was no time or energy for anything else.

She had not been getting any.

She had been getting *less* than usual.

Was the universe punishing her for trying to take Christmas away from Jasper?

"Am I a bad person?" she asked the black kitten plushie she was tucking into the toy box. She'd rescued the plushie from a sodden, falling-down Halloween display the day she met Jasper.

She had been so unhappy then, she'd seen herself in the bedraggled, unwanted toy with one of its eyes missing.

The kitten was in much better shape now. It had been laundered, mended, received state-of-the-art new-eye-surgery, and had even survived being Ruby's favorite plaything since she was old enough to start grabbing at what she wanted.

Abigail was so much happier now, too, but what if underneath it all, she was still that messed-up, gross, slightly stinky cat toy that nobody wanted?

"Mommy!" Ruby bounded into the room. "I'm ready for the party! Ooh, kitty-cat is here! I wanna bring him to the party too!"

Tonight, they were all heading to dinner at one of the local restaurants that was run by a bear shifter family. Jasper had booked out the whole restaurant so that the kids could come out too, and they wouldn't have to stress about a human seeing a tiny dragon or fiery hellpuppy if the kids got too excited and lost control of their shifting.

"Sure he can come, sweetheart."

"He can wear my crown!"

"Who can wear your crown?" Jasper walked in, shrugging on a sweater embroidered with disco-dancing reindeer.

"Kitty-cat!" Ruby hugged the little toy, and Abigail's heart melted.

Jasper put his arm around her. "You okay?" he murmured.

"Why wouldn't I be?"

"Because I just walked in here to find you clutching that little soft toy and looking like you were about to cry?" He searched her face.

She swatted at him. "I wasn't looking like I was about to cry!"

"I could have taken a photo and put it on a fundraiser. We would have made millions." He pulled her close and kissed her. "Really, are you feeling all right? I know Christmas isn't the easiest time for you, that's why I—"

"Mommy Daddy look!" Ruby rushed to the window. "Auntie Opal and Uncle Hank are here already! It's time to go!"

Abigail tossed the toy to Ruby, who caught it with a squeal, and leaned into him. He was warm and sturdy, the sweater was surprisingly soft despite all the sequins, and...

She took a deep breath.

"It's nothing," she said. "Just getting stuck in my own head." *Worrying that really you're fine, everything's fine, and I'm the one who's going to ruin Christmas because… I'm a grinch who doesn't want anyone to be happy?*

She'd gotten it all the wrong way around. Everyone loved Christmas. *Jasper* loved Christmas. Why would he keep trying to do more and better Christmas-y things if it was making him unhappy?

Didn't it make more sense for the unhappiness she felt in the mate bond to be… her?

Another deep breath. This one tasted like guilt.

There were only a few days left until Christmas. It was time to stop ruining everyone's day.

"I'm fine," she said, determined to make it true.

No more scheming. No more plans.

Jasper deserved a happy Christmas. He deserved better than her ruining it.

6

JASPER

His mate was hurting. And she was *lying* about it.

Something like panic gripped him as they all headed to dinner, and it still had him in its claws when they returned home. It didn't let go, all that night or the next.

Everything he'd been doing to make this Christmas the best year ever, to make things magical and wonderful and perfect? It hadn't worked. He needed to—to—

Try harder. Do *even better.*

And he had one last chance to do it.

Christmas Eve.

Tonight.

7

ABIGAIL

Jasper didn't say anything else about her looking downcast, which was both good, and made her feel even guiltier. What would she have said to him, anyway? *I thought you were stressing out over Christmas too much, so I roped my friends into stealing away all your Christmas fun, and that only made you seem MORE stressed, and I'm the one who's going to ruin Christmas because underneath it all, it turns out I'm a grinch who doesn't want anyone to be happy?*

She bit her lip.

It was Christmas Eve. That evening, they were heading to the skating rink a short distance out of town. The lake was a popular swimming and boating spot in summer, but over winter it became something truly magical. A field of glittering ice surrounded by a snowy forest, looking out over the mountainside with the stars blazing overhead.

There was a little island in the middle of the lake. In summer, people swam out to it. In winter, the few trees that grew on it were a last-ditch refuge for skaters who needed something to cling onto if they got unsteady out on the ice.

So far as she knew, there were no special events planned there for this Christmas Eve. Just a quiet evening, and a chance to let Ruby wear herself out so she might get to sleep before midnight.

Jasper kneeled to help Ruby with her skates. "Remember, if you feel unsteady, or think you're going too fast, just aim at me. I'll catch you." His eyes flicked up to focus on Abigail's, and fire stirred in their gemstone-colored depths. "The same goes for you."

"I like to think I'm *slightly* better at skating these days," she said with a wince.

"But if you do…" His voice trailed off, and he opened his arms invitingly as he stood up. Her wince turned into a smile that was far more suggestive than she meant it to be.

"I'll wait until we're in a dark corner and then trip you up?" She stood on tip-toe to whisper as close to his ear as she could reach, and his pupils darkened. "Sounds perfect."

"No you can't, Daddy, because you'll be busy!" Ruby piped up. "With the surprise!"

Jasper's eyes widened. Abigail's heart thudded.

"Surprise?" she asked.

Jasper bit the inside of his cheek. She stared at him. It was almost as though he'd forgotten whatever he had planned. Like he'd been so into the idea of just going skating as a family that whatever big surprise he had up his sleeve had slipped his mind, and it was a surprise for himself, as well?

No, that didn't make any sense.

"Right," he said, laughing weakly. "I guess I won't be able to play safety mat if I'm busy with the, uh, surprise."

"Abigail, Jasper, there you are!" Sheena waved as she walked over to them, Fleance and a few other members of the hellhound pack in tow. "Happy Christmas Eve! Any plans for it?"

"We're here for skating, hot cocoa, and a few photos under the trees, that's the whole plan. Because we've gotta be back home and in bed early for Santa, right?" Jasper winked at Ruby.

"Yeah!" Ruby agreed, and then looked suddenly worried. "Daddy, if we're home too late does that mean Santa won't come?"

"Certainly not," Jasper reassured her. But there was a slightly distant look in his eye that made Abigail… concerned.

"Mommy, can I play with Cole and the others before we go skating?" Ruby tugged at her sleeve, and Abigail looked across to where her tweenaged nephew, Cole, was clearly tallying up all the extra allowance he was going to bargain for in exchange for hanging out with a hoard of small children. They were hanging out near the hot drinks stand, throwing snowballs at him.

"Olly and Meaghan are watching them too," Sheena pointed out, and Abigail told Ruby she could go.

It wasn't that she didn't trust Cole. The poor kid had two solid years of quelling Ruby's schemes on his resume. But one not-yet-teenaged boy watching three shifter kids who all had innate fire magic felt like bad odds.

Jasper sighed and picked up Ruby's abandoned skates. Abigail nudged him. "It's better than her getting frustrated with how slow skating is and deciding she wants to fly around the ice instead, isn't it?"

"Good point." He gave a wry smile. "If the others are happy watching her, maybe we could—"

"Hey Jasper, Fleance and Caine were looking for you before. Something about… a scheme?" Sheena suggested with an innocent grin.

Panic flashed across Jasper's face. He kissed Abigail and left. Quickly.

The moment Jasper was gone, Sheena sat down next to Abigail and leaned to whisper in her ear, "That was *not* the face of a man who has no secret plans up his sleeve."

Abigail groaned. "You saw it too?"

"Don't worry. We got the guys on board. Fleance and Caine have it covered. But what about you? What happened to your plan?" At Abigail's confused stare, she elbowed her. "Come on! How many chances have we given you to slope off with Jasper and get some you-time in, and you keep just… How do I put this…" She raised both hands to shape quotes in the air. "'Taking part in fun Christmas activities'? 'Enjoying quality family time'?"

"I don't *hate* Christmas," Abigail said hurriedly.

"Sure, but that's what you were after… wasn't it? So, what's the problem? Because my plan here was to boot Jasper over to the guys so they could get his latest scheme out of him and send him back here, while Meaghan and I keep your super-cute kid out of the way so that you two can quietly disappear by yourselves…?" She trailed off, one eyebrow raised suggestively, and then frowned. "But why do I get the feeling that isn't going to happen? Come on, Abigail. It's Christmas Eve. This is your last chance to get away before the big day."

"You got the guys on board, too?" Abigail asked helplessly.

"Well, yeah. I mean, I personally am not so sneaky that Fleance didn't immediately notice how sneaky I was being. Delphine can't lie to Hardwick without him getting a headache about it. Plus, it turns out that Jasper had already asked them all for help making this the best Christmas ever anyway, so—"

"Wait, Jasper asked for their help?" Abigail's eyes flew across the square to where her husband was chatting with his friends. "He's been scheming, too?"

"…Yes? But it means they were already on board with turning things up to eleven, so…"

"Oh no."

Sheena frowned. "Oh *no*?"

"All this extra Christmas isn't just business as usual? It's part of something he's planning deliberately?"

And the more she meddled, the more extra Jasper got.

The more *unhappy* she felt about it, the harder he tried.

To make this the biggest, best Christmas ever.

"I got this all wrong," she gasped. "I have to talk to him."

8

JASPER

"What if, after the kids have a chance to play a bit, we—"

Look out, Abigail's coming up right behind you. Caine raised his hand to wave. "Hi, Abigail! Happy Christmas Eve!"

"Happy almost-Christmas to you, too. Will you all be coming by the lodge tomorrow afternoon?"

"Wouldn't miss it. Looking forward to letting the twins gnaw on someone else's furniture for once."

"Maybe they can chew off the scorch marks Ruby left last time we visited," Abigail grinned.

Caine winced. "Don't let them hear you say that. They'll think it's a great idea." He clapped Jasper on the shoulder. "We'd better get onto it, then!"

Onto what? Jasper asked, exasperated. *I haven't told you the plan yet!* The fake plan, that was. The plan that would keep his so-helpful friends busy while he pulled off the *real* plan. The one that would make all of this worth it.

The plan that… meant he would be busy carrying out the plan this evening, instead of skating around the icy lake and watching Ruby screech with delight.

Instead of letting Abigail fall into his arms.

Uncertainty prickled at him.

Caine winked and sauntered off with Fleance, leaving Jasper and Abigail alone.

"Why do I get the feeling we're being deliberately abandoned?" Jasper wondered. He quirked a smile down at Abigail. "And it's not the first time this has happened."

She smiled, wincing. "You noticed?"

"That everyone in my life is doing their best to steal Christmas from me?"

"That isn't—" Abigail's face fell, and his heart dropped with it. "I'm not—it wasn't—"

"That was a joke," he said quickly, and took her shoulders to bring her to face him. "Sweetheart, what's wrong?"

She sighed, and Jasper and his inner dragon both tensed. "Nothing's wrong. I just—"

Alarm bells rang in his head.

Abigail was his fated mate. The other half of his soul. His *wife.* There should be no *I just,* with that closed-in expression on her face, like she was trying to lock away whatever she was feeling.

Guilt turned a back-flip inside him. Of all times of the year, this should be the best, and he'd been doing his best to make sure it was.

He should have tried harder.

"I'll make it up to you," he promised.

Her frown deepened. "No, that's what I wanted to talk to you about—"

*DADDY!*ance* Ruby wailed in his head.

Jasper flinched. Abigail paled and put a hand to her chest. "Was that Ruby?"

Abigail wouldn't have heard Ruby's telepathic cry—but she must have felt his jolt of shock through the mate bond.

"Yes." He turned in the direction he'd last seen Ruby. The play area by the snow-fight zone was empty. *Bee-bee, where are you?*

The surprise went wrong!

"What's happening? Where did they go?" Abigail asked urgently.

He grabbed her hand and repeated Ruby's message.

"Surprise? What—oh no."

She ran, tugging him with her, towards the frozen lake.

The beautiful, serene, sparkly lake of ice. With its tiny island in the middle.

Which was on fire.

Neither of them had their skates on yet. They sprinted and skidded across the ice. Jasper's dragon fought to transform, but he wouldn't let it. There were humans here who didn't know that shifters existed.

And adding another panicked, fire-breathing creature to the situation was not going to help.

HELLHOUNDS! he yelled. *WE NEED SOME FIREFIGHTING OVER HERE!*

Uncle Jasper! another voice wailed.

Cole, what the hell is going on?

They dumped a load of snow on me and disappeared!

"I thought Meaghan and Olly were watching them!" Abigail panted.

"So did I." He caught her as her feet skidded from under her, and then they were on the island.

There were three lonely pine trees on this stupid island, and they were all on fire. Heat seared against his face and snow crunched under his feet as he searched for the kids. Ruby and the others' psychic signatures were here somewhere, but—

There!

Three tiny faces turned to theirs, bathed in flickering firelight. Ruby's face was pale with fright.

The two hellpuppy twins were alight with glee.

"Ruby!" Abigail rushed past him and scooped up their daughter. Jasper grabbed the twins, hurrying them further away from the fire. The blaze had truly caught by now.

And then, just as quickly, it died.

Sheena jogged to a halt next to them, hands still raised as she used her hellsheep magic to quell the fire. "What the *fu*—" she began, and glanced guiltily at the kids. "I mean, what the—he—uhh—shi—*jiminy crickets,*" she said at last, with feeling.

The others ran up, but the emergency was over. Meaghan and Caine scooped the twins away, and the ice running through Jasper's veins melted.

"I didn't mean for it to do that, Daddy!" Ruby wailed. "I wanted it to be special!"

Something pulsed through the mate bond from Abigail's heart to his—relief, mixed with something like regret. And understanding.

"Hot cocoa," he announced out loud. "And then the four of you can tell us all how that happened."

It took multiple mugs of hot cocoa, each one topped with more marshmallows until the last mug was more marshmallow than drink. But eventually the kids were ready to talk.

"I know I was meant to be watching them," Cole said miserably. "But they knocked the snowman on top of me and—I swear it only took a minute for me to get out, and then—"

"HeeheeheeHEEHEE," the twins cackled in unison. Caine and Meaghan looked drained.

"*I* was meant to be watching you all," Meaghan said, rubbing her forehead. She looked up at Caine. "I only looked away for a moment, helping Cole out of the snow…"

Her mate cupped her face. "I know how fast they are."

"*I* know how fast they are." She sighed. "I used to think a whole pack to two shifter kids was a safe ratio. Guess I was wrong about that."

Behind her, Sheena and Fleance exchanged a silent grimace, and Sheena ghosted her hand over her midsection.

If that meant what Jasper thought it meant… then he agreed with them that right now was not a good time to tell their alphas that the ratio might soon be *three* shifter kids against a pack of adults.

Ruby scooped up a slug of melted marshmallow and spooned it into her mouth.

"Are you ready to tell us now?" Abigail asked gently.

"I wanted to do a special Christmas surprise too," Ruby told them in the tiniest voice Jasper had ever heard from her. She reached into her pocket and pulled out handful after handful of Christmas decorations Jasper had never seen before. Macaroni stars, glittery cardboard trees, an extremely squashed length of bunting…

"Did you make these?" he asked.

Ruby nodded, and sniffed. "I wanted to go all the way over the ice to the island and make a Christmas tree for you and Mommy. And I did! I got all the way there! But Lola and Hamish came too and… then they…" She sniffed harder. "THEY started the fire! It wasn't me!"

Jasper exchanged a glance with Abigail, then looked at the twins. They were both still in unrepentantly good moods.

As they watched, a patch of the picnic table in front of them started to smolder.

Caine smacked his hand over it to put it out. "I believe you," he told Ruby. "These little firebugs get too excited, and, well… you've seen the consequences."

"And THEN," Ruby continued, glowing with vindication. "And THEN, they…" Her face darkened. "*Hmph.*"

She refused to say any more.

9

ABIGAIL

After that, everyone was more than ready to go home.

The drive back to their house was somber. Ruby was exhausted and upset by her failed Christmas surprise. She perked up after they set up a new Christmas tree in the front room specifically for her decorations, but Abigail and Jasper's nerves were still frazzled by the time she went off to bed.

"That could have gone badly," she said as they headed back downstairs after putting Ruby to bed.

"Worse than it actually did?" Jasper had a far-off look in his eyes. "I didn't realize she'd been planning something. Do you think…"

"That all your plans rubbed off on her?" Abigail gave a weak smile. "Don't take all the blame. You weren't the only one plotting."

"I wasn't?"

It was time to come clean.

She took a deep breath.

"Momm-yyyy…" A soft wail drifted down the stairs.

She turned back to the stairs. "I'll go see what that's about."

"Dad-dyyy…"

"Sounds like I'm coming with you."

Ruby was waiting for them, sitting upright in bed, a determined and slightly damp expression on her face.

"What's wrong, sweetie?" Abigail asked, sitting beside her and pulling her into a cuddle.

Ruby sniffled against her shoulder. "Does Santa Claus really not bring presents if you've been bad?"

Abigail exchanged a look with Jasper. "Well…"

"What if you do something wrong but it's already really late… if he's already packed the presents, does he still give them to you? Or does he throw them away?"

"You haven't done anything wrong, Bee-bee," Jasper told her, patting her hair.

"It's not ME," she said, outraged. "Hamish and Lola… They did…" Her voice faded into a muffled whisper.

"I'm sure they didn't mean to set the tree on fire," Jasper said.

Abigail was less sure, but she kept quiet.

"Remember when you used to accidentally set things on fire? And Santa Claus always brought you presents, because he knew it was an accident," Jasper said reassuringly.

"They did it on PURPOSE. And they were YUCKY," Ruby grumped. "And then they LAUGHED."

"What did they laugh about?" Abigail asked.

Ruby looked disgusted. "You're not allowed to tell anybody."

"Okay…?"

"*Or* Santa."

"I promise."

Ruby looked around, as though worried someone else might be listening in. She pulled Abigail's head close and whispered damply in her ear, "They did WEES and then they set the WEES on FIRE."

Abigail went perfectly still. This was serious business.

If she laughed, Ruby would be *very upset.*

"That was… very cheeky of them," she managed to say at last.

Jasper looked confused. He must not have heard the whisper.

"I never did that!" Ruby stuck her chin out.

"Nope. You never did." *And I didn't know just how lucky I was,* Abigail added silently.

Ruby's expression changed to one of mercenary hopefulness. "Does that mean I get more presents? Because I never set my wees on fire?"

Jasper burst into a coughing fit.

"We'll see," Abigail said firmly. "It's getting late. If Santa's going to have time to reach our house you'll need to get some sleep now, won't you?"

Jasper was still coughing when they kissed her goodnight and left the room. He clicked the door shut behind him and sagged against it, sliding slowly to the floor.

"Of all the things I never knew I had to be grateful for," he groaned. "I thought little girls were sugar and spice and all things nice?"

"Sugar and spice and mass destruction." Abigail sat next to him, her back against the door. "Are there any kids in our group who *aren't* going to be firebugs from birth?"

"Don't tell the alphas just yet, but I think Sheena's pregnant."

"You noticed that too?" She took his hand, twining her fingers through his. "Sheena's baby will be part sheep shifter…"

"And part hellhound. Which makes me think hell-lamb. Another checkmark for the firebug column, either way."

She hummed. "Olly and Jackson are maybe going to start trying soon. I don't think owls *or* pegasi are known for their pyromania."

"Ditto griffins and winged lions. So, there is hope. Eventually, the local kids will stop trying to burn things down." He rested his head against hers.

"Or they'll have to start trying harder."

"Please, I'm trying to stay positive!"

"We need some friends with ice-magic to balance it out. Put that in the tourist brochures."

Jasper laughed. "It's the twenty-first century. I'll put it in the tourist TikToks. With rizz."

"With what?"

"You know, I actually have no idea."

"Oh god. It's finally happened. I'm too old for slang."

"You're perfect." He lifted his head. She looked up to find him gazing down at her, his eyes like a banked fire. Her heart thudded. "And I'm an idiot for not doing this sooner."

He lowered his head and kissed her.

Not one of the quick hello or goodbye kisses they exchanged as automatically as making coffee in the morning. Not a goodnight kiss or a quick peck on the way past. A long, slow, passionate kiss that sent ripples over her skin and made her toes curl.

His hand came up to her face, cupping and caressing, holding her gently as he explored her mouth with his lips, his tongue, his teeth. She melted against him.

Maybe her plans had worked, after all.

"So." Jasper leaned back, surveying her with heat-filled eyes and an expression of mischievous satisfaction. "I hear you've been scheming against me?"

She was still light-headed. "And *you've* been scheming against my schemes!"

"In my defense, I didn't know you were scheming. Had I known, I would have acted differently."

"You would have schemed more cunningly?"

"Maybe I wouldn't have schemed at all."

She pressed her lips together, searching his eyes, and found the same thing she always did: more love than she'd thought existed in the whole world, all in this man, and all for her.

Her heart somersaulted.

"Don't say that," she complained with a grimace. "Then I might start to think we could have talked about this whole thing like sensible people, and we *both* know that neither of us is sensible when it comes to Christmas."

He gave a wry smile. "Good point. You're right. I probably would have listened to everything you said, and then schemed even *more* subtly to achieve the best Christmas ever without you noticing."

"Don't make me tie you up with tinsel to save you from yourself."

"Being tied up was an option?" His eyes gleamed. "You know, I just remembered, I have a whole extra project I need to work on right now—"

She grabbed him as he pretended to stand up, and they both stifled laughter.

"I wouldn't dare," he reassured her. "Even for the promise of being tied up with tinsel."

"Really? It's so *wiry*. And the shiny bits would all flake off and get everywhere…"

"Stop, you're turning me on."

She giggled, and nestled against him. "All right. Who gave it away?"

"The schemes?"

"Mmm."

He stroked her hair. "Nobody."

"Then how did you—"

"You tried to confess what you'd been up to a few times. Once I began to put the pieces together, that suggested you had something to confess to." His hand reached the nape of her neck, and he massaged the tight muscles there. "And then I began to get suspicious. I knew what *I* was scheming. The biggest, best Christmas ever. But somehow every time I got something started, someone grabbed it and ran away with it."

"Didn't you ask your friends to help you out?"

"Help me out, yes. Leave me with nothing to do except spend time with my wonderful mate…" The warmth in his eyes was tinged with regret. "It's so obvious in retrospect. I've been a complete idiot, haven't I?"

She grimaced. "We're well matched, then. I admit it. I got my friends to sabotage all of your new schemes. I mean, I guess all our friends worked together to do it, by the end."

"Terrible. It's almost as though they want us to be happy."

Her stomach squirmed. "But… that's *why* I did it. I thought I sensed you being *unhappy* through the mate bond. There was something there—some stress, or tension, and I thought it must have to do with all the extra Christmas stuff you were planning. I wanted you to take some time off. Sheena and Meaghan and the others thought I just wanted more date nights with you around our anniversary, that's why they—and I know I was wrong, but—"

His forehead creased. "You weren't wrong."

"I wasn't?"

He shook his head. "You saw through me better than I saw myself." He kissed her, gently as a snowflake. "I'm sorry I messed up all your date night schemes."

"I'm sorry I tried to sabotage your life's work instead of have a simple conversation." She bit her lip, and Jasper's eyes caught on the movement. "And it's not like I took advantage of all the opportunities the others made for me to whisk you away, anyway. Just spending time with you and Ruby when you weren't running around was the perfect lead-up to Christmas."

"Something I feel like I should have known, instead of focusing on the running-around part." Jasper ran his fingertips along her shoulder. "But, you know… we're not completely out of time."

He nodded at the closed door they were both leaning against. "You think she'll sleep all night?"

"I don't think she's asleep *now*."

They both listened to their daughter singing carols to herself in bed until her voice slowed as she drifted off and the house was filled with silence.

Jasper took her hand. "Remember our first Christmas?"

"How could I forget? It was the Christmas I found out dragons existed. The Christmas I learned there was more to Christmas than being yelled at and hoping for the sort of holiday that only happens in the movies." Her eyes grew misty. "The Christmas I met you."

"I thought it would be my last Christmas." Jasper's voice tightened. "That my family curse would catch up with me, and I wouldn't have anything to show for my life except years wasted hunting for something that didn't exist, instead of spent with my family in the time I had. And I would spend the rest of my days only half of myself, losing either my dragon or my human side forever. Instead it was the Christmas I found love. The Christmas the tragedy of my life turned into happiness." He reached up to cup her face. "The Christmas I found you. And my life did change forever, for the better."

He paused. "I think I've spent every Christmas since then trying to top it."

"You noticed?" she teased him gently. "You know, for a while there, everyone thought you were going to step back. You actually managed it one year, remember?"

He gave a wry smile. "One year was enough to give me anxiety. I couldn't let you think that meeting me was the highlight of our lives. I had to show you that every year would be better. That even though you'd been alone before, from now on and every year after, you'd always be surrounded by people who loved you."

"And what about pulling back, when the celebrations became ridiculous?"

"How could I pull back from showing you how much I love you?"

She took him in—all of him. The love and warmth in his eyes, the strength in the hand that was holding hers, the softness of his palm against her cheek.

This man who'd seen every sad, unhappy part of her behind the spiky armor she'd worn for so long she thought it was a part of herself, and made it his mission to turn the world into something that would fill her heart.

"Easy," she told him. "You let me show you how much I love *you.*"

10

JASPER

He was an idiot, obviously. But eventually, the most obvious things made it into even his thick head.

Such as the fact that he could never have given his mate her best Christmas ever by keeping so busy they didn't have any time for each other.

He and Abigail crept down the hallway, giggling like teenagers trying not to get caught. His foot caught on a stray decoration—he didn't look, but it clonked like one of the nutcrackers Abigail had banished for looking too creepy. The sound echoed down the hallway and they both froze, clutching one another, suddenly feeling like intruders in their own house.

Jasper met Abigail's eyes. He only meant it as a glance; a knowing wink, a wry comment about Christmas coming for them in the form of an army of poorly designed Nutcracker dolls.

Her face was flushed. Her eyes danced with excitement—and frustration, and a trace of wariness because what if Ruby woke up, and amusement because here was that damn Nutcracker, *again,* and all of a sudden he saw what wasn't there.

The anxiety. The worry. The tension and stillness that had haunted him and his dragon for the last month.

She gazed up at him, and everything else in her eyes melted away into a love that burned like the sun and wrapped warm arms around his soul. "That stupid doll," she muttered, and her voice did delicious things to him. "I thought I threw it out."

"You never throw anything out. You feel too sorry for them." He leaned her against the wall, brushing hair off her face. "Any poor little—"

And then, just as he still teasing her and himself into things, she got in first and kissed him.

The press of her lips to his, the nuzzle of her nose, the way she lifted one hand and touched the tips of her fingers to the edge of his jaw, tracing the bristles of his beard up to the ticklish spot by his ear—his body responded, and he kissed her back the way she liked best, holding her as her knees trembled.

When he finally released her, she gasped in a way that made the mate bond flare.

"Poor little what?" she demanded, eyes bright, challenging and exhilarated.

"Poor little dragon, lost in the snow?" he suggested.

"Poor little Halloween cat, stuck up on the roof." Her mouth curved into a smile of bittersweet kindness. "Waiting for someone to take her home. No wonder I can't throw out any other horrible toys."

"That sounds like a challenge."

Before she could respond, he hitched his arms under her ass, lifting her up and holding her close against him. He could bury his face in her chest—or look up into the face of his mate, worshipful and with a promise he fully intended to keep.

She blushed. *Holy Christmas.* Six years, and he could still make his mate blush like she'd never been looked at this way before.

Six years is nothing, his dragon rumbled. *She's ours forever. And we are hers.*

His voice caught in his throat. When he finally managed to speak, the words came out rough-edged. "I'll always take you home."

"I'm already there."

"Oh, well, in that case, I'll take you to bed."

If any other stray decorations tried to stop them on their way to the bedroom, he didn't notice. They tumbled through the door together, almost slamming it behind them and then turning as one to grab it and close it slowly, gently, *silently.*

They looked at each other as the door clicked shut, and a spark flew between them. Literally.

"Careful," Abigail breathed. "We've had enough wildfires for one night."

"I'll be good," Jasper promised, and his mate's eyes flooded black with desire.

"Does that mean I get to be naughty?"

She led him towards the bed and he stumbled back obediently, feeling as though his feet weren't even touching the ground.

Eyes alight with mischief, she pressed one finger in the center of his chest and pushed. He let himself fall. The bed caught him like a cloud.

Abigail took her time in following him. She stood at the end of the bed, leaning to plant her hands on his thighs. Her sweater neckline hung down, giving a glimpse of warm curves he wanted to touch.

She slid her hands up, just an inch, but enough to make his body harden to rock.

He pushed himself up onto his elbows. "Tell me what you want."

"What? Talk things through, like mature adults?" She straightened, slowly, her hands drifting off his thighs with tantalizing slowness. "That doesn't sound like us."

"That seems harsh. We each wanted to make the other happy."

"And there's nothing wrong with that, except when it turns into a ridiculous slideshow of bad decisions." She played with the hem of her sweater long enough that his fingers itched to tear it off her, then got onto the bed, straddling him on her knees. "Help me with this?"

"Gladly." He snuck his fingers under her sweater and smoothed his palms over her warm skin, brushing his thumbs over the dips of each hip where he knew it would make her tighten with anticipation. She moaned gently and hitched her hips forward.

Beneath the sweater she was all soft curves and warmth, and oh, shit, she was wearing the snowflake-patterned bra he'd bought her a few years ago. He made a low growl deep in his throat and she laughed.

"What?"

"Why did I waste my time with tree decorating schemes this year when I should have bought you more lingerie?"

She laughed again, which was perfect, because laughter shaking her body made her look even better.

He wanted to bury himself in her. Face, dick, it didn't matter; he wanted to press his body to her, wanted to make her shake and quiver and come until she was panting and flushed.

"What are you thinking?" Abigail's voice broke through his sudden rush of desire, pinning it as surely as she was pinning him between her legs. She pressed a hand against her heart, where she always felt her end of their mate bond. "I could… *feel* that. I thought I was meant to be the naughty one?"

He grinned. "I was thinking about being very *nice* to you."

"Oh?"

He pushed her sweater the rest of the way off and threw it aside, taking the opportunity to whisper in her ear and then to kiss his way down to her lips.

"How much I want you. How I want to make you feel good. And that I know exactly how to do it…" He kissed her, open-mouthed and hungry, while his hands undid her trousers and pushed them far enough down to cup her ass. She made a small gasp of pleasure. "I know what you want. Let me give it to you."

"Me, first."

She drew back, biting her lip in a way that stole all his attention.

"You first?" he repeated, a beat too late.

"Yes." She pushed him down, both hands flat against his chest, until she had him where she wanted him and let them drift lower. She undid each button of his shirt, tousling the trail of red-gold hair that led down to the waistband of his pants. "Let me give you something, first."

She pulled his cock out with gentle firmness, wrapping her fingers around him with possessive intent. Fireworks exploded at the back of his mind.

Abigail flicked her eyes up to meet his, dark and wicked behind her long lashes. "I *did* want you to relax for the holidays," she said, mock-apologetic and unrepentant. "But I also wanted this."

She lowered her mouth onto him, kissing the tip of his cock with a lazy deliberation that made his fingers curl into fists at his sides. She dipped her head to suck him in, and the tight heat of her lips and mouth made him black out briefly.

She knew him so well. Knew exactly the pressure and speed and slow, teasing licks…

"Oh *god*," he gasped, and she raised smiling eyes to meet his.

"You've been so *busy*," she complained innocently, licking open-mouthed from the base of his cock to the tip. "And I know I said I wanted to stop you to help you relax, but honestly?"

She licked down the other side, and he felt himself go glassy-eyed.

"It was about *this*, as well. I wanted us to have a happy Christmas… but I want you all to myself, too."

She closed her eyes and took him in, humming contentedly.

Jasper had no words. Fire blazed through his veins as he watched his mate enjoying herself pleasuring him. He wanted her, too—but letting her take what she wanted from him, and give back pleasure ten-fold?

The golden bond between them glowed, passion meeting and twining together with the love that had grown stronger each year they'd been together, and not for the first time Jasper wondered how the hell he got so lucky.

"I love you," he gasped out, and Abigail looked up at him again.

"I've never doubted it." She kissed his tip again. "Do you want to finish this way?"

Her eyes were full of promise, and she had his cock in her hands. It was a promise she knew how to keep.

And he would enjoy every moment of it.

"I told you what I want." He sat and pulled her into his arms, kissing her and tasting himself on her lips.

"You want to make me feel good. Believe me, I feel *very* good."

"And I can't try to improve on that?"

He rolled on top of her, shedding his own clothes so there was nothing between them. She was warm, but he was a blazing fire; she'd taken possession of him, confident in her right to his pleasure, and now it was his turn. He was a dragon, and she was his greatest treasure.

He slipped one hand between her legs. She was hot and wet, and he gave her the heel of his hand to press against, soaking in her desire.

"Tease," she grumbled, rolling her hips. Her breath dragged out in a ragged gasp as she found the pressure she loved.

"How am I the tease?"

"You know I want more than this."

"Mmm," he relented, moving against her. He slid the tip of his cock along her entrance, glorying in how wet she was. She moaned, and the sound tugged at his lust. He wanted more of that noise. He wanted every part of her.

And…

"I want to see you come first," he whispered.

"Th-that won't be a problem," she reassured him, trapping laughter behind gritted teeth.

"Is that so?" He moved so she was settled against his length, slick and hot against his hard need. "Show me."

She flung her head back with a sigh of mingled need and relief, one leg flung over his waist and the other braced against the mattress, holding his hips still as she ground herself against him. She was spectacular. Her breaths came faster, little whining gasps that made him thrust without thinking, and her eyes flew open as she came.

"Ahh-h!"

He swallowed her cry with a deep kiss, arranging himself at her entrance and thrusting in with one slick movement as her body still bucked and trembled with the force of her orgasm. He rode her through the aftershocks, lost in the sweet tight heat of her.

Need drove through him, and the tenor of Abigail's moans changed as he sped up. She met him movement for movement, and when he finally spilled inside her she came again, too, and each gasp made his own pleasure burn brighter.

His mate. His wife. His partner through life. As they lay together afterwards, sweaty and satisfied; as they crept to the shower, washed and kissed and fooled around until they both tumbled into bed again, to sleep this time, one thought drifted contentedly through his mind.

Fate had found them for each other.

He looked at her, lying in his arms, already asleep. One hand curled across his chest, possessive even in sleep.

The mate bond pulsed quietly, a beat connecting their hearts and souls.

That was magic. But the rest of their life together? Fate had nothing to do with it. Their life, their happiness, was theirs to build.

Together.

Which was the greatest magic of all.

Christmas Day was everything it should be. A crisp pale sky hung above fresh, fluffy snow. Ruby woke with a shriek of delight and flung herself downstairs. Jasper grinned into his pillow as he mentally tracked her footsteps through the house until she skidded to a halt in front of the Christmas tree.

He tensed.

The Christmas tree. The *presents*—

He shot upright, and Abigail flung an arm around him and dragged him back into bed. "I put the presents out."

"What? When?"

"Not sure. Sometime after I wore you out so thoroughly you slept like a Yule log all night?"

Abigail had the perfect bedhead and the perfect sleepy, smug smile and the perfect dancing happy eyes. He kissed her until something hit him in the head.

"Stop KISSING! It's CHRISTMAS!" Ruby roared. "I got your STOCKINGS!"

Abigail rolled out from underneath him and caught her own stocking before it smacked her in the face. She adjusted the strap of her cami and Jasper was struck by a sudden, vivid memory of her slipping into it the night before. And out of it. When had she put it on again?

"Happy Christmas, sweetheart," she laughed at Ruby as their daughter clambered onto the bed, so excited that scales shimmered on her cheekbones and forehead. There was no risk she would shift, though—not when she had her own Christmas stocking clutched safely in one hand. "And happy Christmas to you, my love," she told Jasper. Their eyes met, and he felt like he was falling in love all over again. "What's the plan for today?"

"For today? What day is it?" he asked, his forehead crumpling in a way he knew both the ladies in his life found equal parts adorable and unbelievably irritating.

"It's CHRISTMAS DAY!" Ruby and Abigail replied in unison, Ruby shrieking with disbelief, Abigail dissolving into laughter.

"What? Already?" He raised his hands to defend himself from a pillow attack. "All right! I surrender! Happy Christmas!"

With her father properly put in his place, Ruby got on with the important business of doling out gifts from each of their stockings. Jasper and Abigail oohed and ahhed over the knick-knacks and random snacks they'd each hinted to the other that they would like, and gasped in genuine delight at the few secret gifts they'd each managed to sneak into the stocking haul.

"As for plans," Jasper said, pulling Abigail close. "Let's just say I suspect our friends have something up their sleeves."

When the stockings had been scoured of all their secrets, they all headed downstairs. Jasper made waffles and Abigail fussed over coffee and hot chocolate while Ruby kept a watchful eye on the gifts under the Christmas tree, carefully selecting which ones she would ask to open before they put the rest in the car to take up to her aunt and uncle's house.

Jasper's heart melted as he watched her, and the heart-shaped ornament at the top of the tree sparkled in the early morning light coming in through the window. The first gift Abigail had ever given him. The heart of his Christmas hoard, and a reminder of everything they were to each other.

Christmas at Opal and Hank's was an all-hands-on-deck affair. There was lunch, and presents, and afternoon tea, and presents, and a half-hearted attempt at a digestion-settling walk, and presents, and dinner, and music and games and a constant tide of friends and neighbors dropping by. Local shifters, his and Abigail's best friends among them, often found their way to the Heartwell lodge for the privacy and freedom to shift into their animal forms, and Christmas was no different—except the hellhounds and other mythical animals were at risk of being decorated as festively as the Christmas tree if they tried to nap where the kids were playing, or put to work as portable bonfires for toasting marshmallows on.

Night had fallen and the real bonfire was burning merrily in the back courtyard when Abigail snuck up behind him and put her arms around him. "You win after all," she said. "This *is* the best Christmas ever."

"Every Christmas with you is the best Christmas ever," he told her.

"Should I remind you of that when you start to go crazy next year?"

He pulled her around to hug her, resting his chin on top of her head. "Put it in the calendar."

"Will do."

"And I'll put in my calendar, *Remember the love of your life is going to start worrying about you freaking out about Christmas about now.*" He kissed her. "And then—"

He paused, suddenly aware of a hushed whispering behind him. A moment later, the air erupted with cheers.

"Happy birthday!"

He turned, Abigail in his arms. All his friends and family gathered behind him, smiling hugely.

"Oh no," he said jokingly.

"Oh *yes*," Opal announced with a mock-stern expression on her face. "You thought we were going to forget?"

"I—" He looked down at Abigail. "Were you in on this?"

"Did you think *I* was going to forget your birthday?"

"But… it's Christmas…"

"And that isn't the only thing worth celebrating." She tucked her hand into his. "Are you ready for more presents? More songs? More cake?"

He gazed down at her. "More of everything," he said.

There was one surprise left to come. After the surprise birthday party, even the most energetic of the kids were starting to have trouble keeping their eyes open—and some adults, too.

"We'll come back in the morning to help tidy up, but I think it's time we were going," he told Opal.

"Good idea. We've got the spare room set up here for Ruby."

"What?"

His sister raised her eyebrows at him. "Look. How long have I been your sister now?"

"Almost exactly my entire life, except for the week you lived in the tree-stump out back pretending you were a lost mermaid princess?"

"Never tell anyone about that. But yes. Your whole life. So don't think I don't see what's going on here." She sighed deeply, giving him the big-sisterly smile-scowl he knew and loved. "I mean, chances are I *don't*. Obviously, the whole family curse thing plagued us our entire lives, and with the deadline being your birthday and your birthday being *Christmas*, that was weird and stressful, and I guess I never figured out how much of you being crazy over Christmas was legitimate and how much was a reaction to that—"

"Look, sis, I can think of better times to psychoanalyze me—"

"All right, all right. I'm just saying."

"And I do love Christmas. Legitimately."

"Good. And we love you. Legitimately. So, here's your birthday present, little bro. From all of us. Yes, even whoever that is asleep on the porch."

"The party?"

"Nope. This." She thrust an envelope into his hands. "Now go and enjoy it."

Abigail came up beside them. "What's that?" she asked.

"The result of *sisterly* scheming," Opal informed her. "None of this secretive rubbish. Just me straight up ordering my little brother to go on a mini break for his birthday."

"That *works*?" Abigail asked, mock-astonished. "Just telling him things?"

"Well?" Opal asked him.

A grin spread across Jasper's face. "Yes," he said. "It works."

11

ABIGAIL

Abigail was fuzzy with food and drink and the exhaustion of a long, amazing day, but couldn't even think about sleeping. She couldn't drag her eyes off her husband long enough to blink, let alone nap.

Opal and Hank had all but pushed them out of their home after they gave Jasper his birthday present: a night at one of the vacation cottages farther along the valley. Quiet, and remote, and just for the two of them.

They were there now. If Abigail had been capable of looking anywhere but at Jasper, she was sure she would have exclaimed over how adorable it was. She knew what these cottages were like: cozy and quaint and perfect.

But she didn't need to look to know how perfect this was.

"Our friends and your sister got together to do this for us?" she asked as they walked up to the cottage.

"They did."

"Those *fiends*. Don't they know they're meant to plan and scheme things like this?"

"I mean, this was definitely a scheme."

"Just one that worked?"

"*Your* scheme worked." Jasper unlocked the front door. The room beyond was warm, the air scented with a hint of cinnamon. "You got me to stop stressing out about making Christmas the biggest and best ever."

"Barely. At the last possible minute. Anyway, so did yours. Because I don't know if you noticed, but we just had the best Christmas ever."

"Did we?" He frowned adorably. "Because I feel like Christmas isn't over yet."

"It's your birthday now." She tugged him down for a kiss.

"Ohhh," he murmured against her lips. "I see. And this is happy birthday for me?"

"*Yes*," she said firmly. "And—"

Jasper pressed a finger against his lips. "I already know what I want for my birthday," he said, and kneeled in front of her.

She laughed with surprise. "We haven't even closed the door!"

"Close it, then," he retorted, his voice muffled.

She scrambled to shut the door behind them and he wasted no time pushing her against it. She was wearing her outdoor clothes—and then she wasn't, with a speed that made her wonder if Jasper had developed new magical powers.

"Shouldn't we find the bedroom—"

"All in good time."

He pulled her shoes off, then her pants and underwear, and buried his face between her legs. Her knees almost gave out. He huffed amusement and kissed her clit.

Sensation jolted through her. "Jasper!"

"I remember someone asking me to let them enjoy themselves the way they wanted." He looked up at her, and the sight of his eyes dark with lust and love stole all the breath from her lungs. "Won't you let me have my turn now?"

She nodded. She'd *barely* nodded when he picked up one of her legs and placed it over his shoulder. He nuzzled the inside of her thigh. "You're right, though."

"What am I right about?"

"We don't have to rush. We have all the time we need. All this time just for us." He kissed her thigh, slow and worshipful. "No need to rush."

This time, when he put his mouth between her legs, he was so careful and controlled she almost collapsed from anticipation, not shock.

She eased back against the wall, trying not to let her legs shake.

"I should do this every day," he muttered to himself in between licks. "Why don't I do this every day?"

"L-life gets in the way?"

"Life needs to re-prioritize," he declared, and then probably said a few more things. She wasn't listening. She *couldn't* listen. Her body had re-prioritized—all her senses to Jasper's touch, and his mouth, and the little darts of lightning that coiled inside her with every suck and kiss. She ground herself against him, going on tip-toes to get the right angle, to open herself up to him so his tongue could dive deeper, his fingers could find—

She cried out as the coiled lightning inside her struck, again and again. She lost her balance but Jasper was waiting for that. He caught her, holding her tight in his arms until the last shuddering aftershock of orgasm relented and she slumped into his embrace.

He looked entirely too pleased with himself. She mock-scowled and jabbed him in the chest. "We barely got in the door!"

"I know. I'm terrible. I didn't even take my boots off."

"You didn't—" Her eyes widened in actual outrage and he laughed out loud.

"But you're right. We should be sensible about this." He stood up, helping her get to her feet too, and then extravagantly wiped his mouth with a wicked glint in his eye. "We should explore the cottage, first. Make sure we know whether the heating controls are. Check to see if the fridge and pantry are stocked, or whether we need to call for delivery—"

"Absolutely not," Abigail growled. "I've finally got you to myself, we are not calling *anyone* else over to interrupt."

"Even for dinner?"

"We can starve."

He smirked, drawing her into his arms. "I don't think there's any risk of that."

"And we don't need to change the heating. It's plenty warm in here. In fact, if anything, I think you look *too* warm." She tugged on his jacket and dragged it open and down his arms. "We'd better fix that."

"Can't wear my shoes into the house."

"You're the one who left them on!"

When she finally had him more suitable dressed—or rather, undressed—she took her time getting an eyeful.

"Actually, I would like to check out the kitchen," she said, tipping her head to one side. "Give me a minute?"

He caught up with her before she made it three steps, wrapping strong arms around her and laughing into her hair. "I'd prefer to give you something else. But it will take more than a minute."

"Promises, promises."

It took hours. She was sore in the best way, exhausted into bliss, and—though she wouldn't have thought it possible, after the Christmas feast earlier—she was hungry.

They took their time picking out morsels from the fridge. They took their time in the walk-in shower and the bath big enough for two. They laughed, and talked like they hadn't in years, about everything and nothing and redoing their own bathroom with their own massive bath, and relaxed into each other's company as though they had no other cares in the world.

The rest of the world was still out there. Everyone and everything they loved. Ruby, and their friends, and Christmas in Pine Valley. And it would still be there when they left this perfect jewel of a moment of time for themselves.

It was everything she hadn't known she'd needed. Except she had known, hadn't she? Her friends had seen right through her. She wanted Jasper to be happy—and she wanted this. A chance to remind them both of who and what they were for each other, as husband and wife, as fated mates, as two people still disgustingly, deliriously passionate about each other.

She sighed and rested her head on Jasper's chest. They'd found the bedroom, at last. It had taken a while. And several detours. Which was impressive, given the cottage only had about four rooms total, but they'd managed it.

She counted on her fingers—wet room, kitchen, living, bath—okay, with the bedroom that was five, unless you counted the pantry as a separate room…

They'd used their time well, anyway.

She nuzzled against him. "What do you think? Was that a happy enough Christmas for this year? And birthday. Christmabirthday. Birthdaymas."

"More than enough." He kissed her, then turned his head to glance at the clock on the bedside table. "And we still have a few hours left."

"Oh?" She could barely keep her eyes open. "In that case… maybe it *hasn't* been a good enough Birthdaymas."

He laughed. "Who's overworking themselves now?"

"It's not *work…*"

"Rest." He kissed her again, on her lips, on her nose, on her forehead. "It's been perfect. You're perfect. Happy Christmas," he whispered to her. "Thank you for trying to steal it from me."

She let her eyes fall shut. "Happy birthday," she murmured. "Thank you for letting me try to steal it."

She lay in his arms, the most magical place in the world, at the most magical time of the year. Her heart was full to bursting. The future held more joy than she knew what to do with—but with her family, and her friends, that wasn't going to be a problem.

That joy was all of theirs to share, and to make bigger and stronger in all the years to come. Without hiding what they wanted, or what they were worried about. By trusting one another and trusting themselves that they deserved all the love and joy the life they built together would bring them. At Christmas, and every other time of year.

MORE PARANORMAL ROMANCE BY ZOE CHANT

A Mate for Christmas

A Mate for the Christmas Dragon
Christmas Hellhound
Christmas Pegasus
The Hellhound's UnChristmas Miracle
Christmas Griffin

A Gift for the Christmas Dragon (novella)

Shifter Suspense

Claimed by the Panther
Saved by the Billionaire Lion Shifter
Stealing the Snow Leopard's Heart
Craving the Kraken

Falling for the Shadow Dragon
Seducing the Soul-Eater

Hideaway Cove

The Griffin's Mate
The Sea Wolf's Mate
The Lightning Dragon's Mate
The Duskfire Dragon's Mate
The Kelpie's Mate

Standalone books not in series

Her Purr-fect Christmas Mate
Trusting the Tiger
Bear With Me

MONSTER ROMANCE BY MARIE CARDNO

The Monster Girlfriend series

How to Get a Girlfriend (When You're a Terrifying Monster)
How to Get a Date with the Evil Queen
How to Get the Girl (And Not Destroy the World)